Books by Paige Sleuth

Cozy Cat Caper Mystery Series:
Murder in Cherry Hills (Book 1)
Framed in Cherry Hills (Book 2)
Poisoned in Cherry Hills (Book 3)
Vanished in Cherry Hills (Book 4)
Shot in Cherry Hills (Book 5)
Strangled in Cherry Hills (Book 6)
Halloween in Cherry Hills (Book 7)
Stabbed in Cherry Hills (Book 8)
Thanksgiving in Cherry Hills (Book 9)
Frozen in Cherry Hills (Book 10)
Hit & Run in Cherry Hills (Book 11)
Christmas in Cherry Hills (Book 12)
Choked in Cherry Hills (Book 13)
Dropped Dead in Cherry Hills (Book 14)
Valentine's in Cherry Hills (Book 15)
Drowned in Cherry Hills (Book 16)
Orphaned in Cherry Hills (Book 17)
Fatal Fête in Cherry Hills (Book 18)
Arson in Cherry Hills (Book 19)

CHRISTMAS
in CHERRY
HILLS

PAIGE SLEUTH

CHAPTER ONE

"Merry Christmas!" Andrew Milhone said as he lugged a bundle of green into Katherine Harper's apartment.

"You bought a tree already?" Kat planted her hands on her hips. "You were supposed to call me to help pick one out."

"I know, but when I drove by the lot earlier the pickings were getting slim. I wasn't sure there would be any left by the time you got off work."

Kat's jaw dropped open. "Christmas is still two days away, and they're already almost sold out?"

"What can I say, some people plan ahead better than you do."

Kat stuck her tongue out at him.

Andrew adjusted his hold on the trunk. "So where do you want this thing? It's starting to get heavy."

Kat pointed to the space she had cleared next to the living room window. "You can put it over there."

Andrew eyed her. "Some help would be nice."

Matty and Tom, Kat's two cats, evidently thought that was their cue to offer assistance. They both wandered over, turning into a black, brown, and yellow blur as they weaved between Kat's and Andrew's legs in an attempt to get close to the tree.

"You're going to get stepped on," Kat warned them.

The animals weren't concerned, too enraptured by this new addition to their home. Kat accommodated them by shuffling her feet as she made her way across the living room with her end of the tree.

"Tip your side up," Andrew instructed.

Kat did. When she'd raised the tree top as high as she could, Andrew took over, grabbing hold of the side and securing the base of the trunk to the stand. He verified it was steady, then pulled out a pocket knife to snip the twine wrapped around the branches. Matty and Tom watched in awe as the tree unfolded into its full, glorious splendor.

"There!" Andrew brushed his sandy hair away from his eyes. "It fits perfectly."

The burst of joy that seized Kat then took her by surprise. "I never thought I'd ever be looking forward to celebrating Christmas."

Tom didn't waste any time moving in to inspect the pine needles within reach. Matty sat off to the side, her gray-striped tail swishing across the carpet. She stared up at the tree, then crouched low to the ground before springing toward one of the branches. Tom stopped what he was doing to watch as the yellow-and-brown tortoiseshell pulled herself into the tree, her hind feet scrabbling to find a good foothold.

Kat laughed. "I can tell you right now, with Matty and Tom here this Christmas is shaping up to be the best one I've had in all of my thirty-two years."

Andrew slung his arm around Kat's shoulders and kissed her cheek. "I know this will be my best Christmas ever. I have you."

Kat leaned into him, his words making her giddy.

He chuckled. "Look at us getting into the holiday spirit. Remember when we were a couple of kids grumbling about Christmas while everybody else at school couldn't wait to see what kind of loot they were going to be getting?"

"It was different for us. We were in foster care. Christmas isn't much fun when you're sitting around with somebody else's family, opening up generic gifts picked up at the last minute so you don't feel left out. I can't tell you how many times Santa brought me a pair of cheap socks patterned in some kind of reindeer theme."

Kat smiled as Tom swatted at Matty, who was shielded by the branches surrounding her. Matty retaliated by taking a swing at his head. Neither cat made contact, but it was clear they were having a grand time trying.

"They're so cute," Kat said. "I bought some baubles, but now I'm not sure we shouldn't leave the tree as it is. The cats can enjoy it more this way."

Andrew squeezed her shoulder. "It's your tree. You can do whatever you want."

She wrapped her arms around his waist as she rotated toward him. "Thank you for buying it and bringing it over. How much do I owe you?"

He kissed her nose. "Consider it to be a gift."

"We agreed not to exchange gifts."

"Then consider it to be on loan. You can give

it back to me after your mom leaves town."

The reminder that Maybelle Harper was currently on her way to Cherry Hills, Washington sent a flurry of butterflies erupting in Kat's stomach. "I'm nervous about meeting her. What if we don't get along?"

Andrew smirked. "Then you'll be just like every other family."

"I'm serious, Andrew." Kat stepped away from him and flopped onto the couch. "I haven't seen her in twenty-some-odd years. What if we have nothing in common?" *What if she doesn't like me?* was what Kat was really thinking.

Andrew sat down beside her. "You've been talking on the phone, haven't you?"

"We hold five-minute conversations about the weather and how our jobs are going every other week. We don't talk about anything important."

Andrew paused, then said, "Have you told her about me?"

"No," Kat admitted.

"Huh."

Kat could see the disappointment in his eyes, and it twisted her heart. "It's not because I don't want my mother to know we're dating or anything. But when we're on the phone we end up chatting about mundane stuff."

"You've told her about the cats though."

"Yes." Realizing he might think that meant she valued Matty and Tom more than him, she added, "But that's only because she's staying with me for three days. I had to know if she was allergic."

She held her breath, hoping Andrew didn't call her on the lie. The truth was, she often filled her mother in on Matty and Tom's antics just to have something to talk about. Plus, hearing about the cats always made Maybelle laugh.

But if Andrew could tell she was fibbing he didn't let on. "What time is she getting here?" he asked.

"It's a five-hour drive from Estacada, so any minute now."

"Would you like me to leave?"

"What?" Kat sat up. "You mean because my mother's coming?"

"If you don't want her to meet me—"

"No." She laid her hand on his wrist. "It's not like that at all. I'd love for you to be here when she shows up."

Andrew relaxed, a smile breaking out on his face. The sight of his twin dimples sent guilt swirling in Kat's stomach. She hadn't confessed the real reason why she wanted him here, and it wasn't so she could introduce him to her mother as one would a serious boyfriend. It was so he could act as a buffer if things didn't go well between them.

"I don't even know what to call her," Kat said. "She was Maybelle Harper when she lived here. Then there was all that business about her having to flee town and hide out, and now she goes by Kelly Watson."

"You don't call her Mom?"

She shook her head. Although she thought of Maybelle as her mother, 'Mom' suggested a level of familiarity that wasn't there. Maybelle had barely been around during Kat's childhood, and, until recently, she had been completely absent from her adulthood.

"I'll just go with Maybelle," she decided. "That's how I think of her anyway."

The buzzer rang, and Kat's stomach flip-flopped. Maybelle Harper had arrived.

CHAPTER TWO

Maybelle Harper looked just as glamorous in person as she did in the photograph she'd emailed Kat when they'd first reconnected this past summer. Kat had suspected then that the teased-out sable hair, heavy eye makeup, and ruby-red lipstick had been for the benefit of the camera, but now she could see that was her mother's day-to-day look.

"Katherine," Maybelle said, smiling across the threshold, "my baby girl."

Kat smiled back. "Hi, Maybelle."

Disappointment flashed in her eyes. "You know you can call me Mom."

"I know."

The silence stretched between them. Kat flexed her fingers, wondering if she should try for a hug. It seemed like something a mother and daughter would do after reuniting for the first time in two decades. It was actually how Kat had always envisioned a reunion, complete with tears and gushing confessions about how much they loved each other. But as many times as she had dreamed of this moment, now that it was really happening she had no idea what to do.

Maybelle fluffed her hair, and the opportunity was lost. "So, were you going to invite me inside?"

"Oh." Kat held the door open. "Please, come in."

Maybelle breezed into the living room, dragging two huge suitcases behind her. When Kat closed the door, she saw her mother was wearing heels. Had she actually driven all the way from Oregon in those things? Her feet must be killing her.

"Oh, hello." Maybelle stopped short in the middle of the room, her eyes on Andrew. "I didn't realize Katherine had company."

Andrew stood up and held out his hand. "Andrew Milhone."

"Andrew . . ." Maybelle's eyes widened. "You're that scrawny little blond boy who used to run around with Katherine, aren't you?"

Andrew laughed. "Guilty as charged."

Maybelle let go of her luggage and sandwiched his hand between hers. "You've certainly filled out well. If I do say so myself, you're a bona fide hunk."

Kat stilled, not missing how her mother's voice had turned low and throaty. She couldn't be hitting on Andrew, could she? Even if she wasn't aware of his and Kat's relationship, he was still a good twenty years her junior.

When Maybelle finally released Andrew's hand, he slipped it into his pants pocket. "How was the drive?" he asked.

"Long." Maybelle perched on the edge of the sofa armrest and crossed her legs. "But the weather was all right. When I started off this afternoon the skies were looking like snow. Thank stars things cleared up the farther I drove. Snow is nice to look at, but . . ."

Kat's heart sank as her mother droned on. She had hoped they could move past the inconsequential small talk once they were face-to-face, but so far this visit was turning into a repeat of one of their phone conversations.

"Oh, my!" Maybelle jumped away from the couch, her list of most hated weather-related road hazards dying on her lips. "Something's moving in that tree."

"That would be Matty and Tom," Kat replied.

"Your cats?" Maybelle frowned. "I didn't realize they were so . . . disruptive."

"They're just having fun."

Maybelle, Kat, and Andrew watched in silence for a minute as Matty and Tom climbed between branches. Kat wasn't sure exactly what they were trying to accomplish, but they seemed to be enjoying themselves.

"What on earth is a tree doing inside your place?" Maybelle asked Kat.

"It's a Christmas tree."

"But it's bare."

"I bought some ornaments and lights." Kat gestured toward the dining room table. "I was holding off on decorating until Matty and Tom are done playing."

Maybelle's lips puckered. "You're talking like the cats run this house."

Kat kept her mouth shut. That was closer to the truth than she cared to admit.

But Andrew laughed, the traitor. "Matty and Tom are definitely the ones in charge here."

Maybelle's lips curved up as she gave him a once-over. "Oh, now, I find that hard to believe when there's a man as big and strong as you around."

Kat's stomach clenched. Her mother was definitely putting the moves on Andrew.

Maybelle took off her coat, revealing a bright red blouse tucked into her black slacks. "You know what I would do if I were the one in charge?"

"What's that?" Kat asked.

Maybelle tossed her coat on the coffee table and spun toward the dining room. "Decorate that Christmas tree."

"We can't do anything while Matty and Tom are there."

"Andrew." Maybelle batted her eyelashes at him as she picked up a string of lights and started undoing the twist ties holding it together. "Could you be a love and lock those animals away somewhere?"

Andrew glanced at Kat. She stared back at him. When she still hadn't spoken after several seconds passed, he shrugged and walked over to the tree.

"It's nice to have a man around, isn't it?" Maybelle said, ostensibly to Kat although it was Andrew she winked at.

Kat couldn't take it anymore. "Maybelle, there's something I need to tell you."

"What's that?"

"Andrew and I are dating."

Maybelle tossed a twist tie aside. "Well, I know that."

"You do?"

"Naturally. Why else would he be here?"

"We could just be friends."

Maybelle snickered. "No way can a woman just be friends with a stud muffin like that."

Andrew shot Kat a look over his shoulder. Maybelle seemed to have left him half amused, half bewildered.

Kat knew exactly how he felt. Her mother was making her head spin. If she knew Andrew was off-limits, why had she been flirting with him?

She never would have guessed Maybelle was such a tease. Although, maybe her surprise was unwarranted. After all, it wasn't as if the topic had ever come up during one of their discussions about the weather.

Kat tried to remember if Maybelle had been this flirtatious twenty years ago but drew a blank. She had probably been too young to notice.

Andrew extricated Matty from the tree first. "I'll put her in the bedroom," he said to Kat as the tortoiseshell squirmed in his arms.

With his sister gone, the tree's appeal faded in Tom's eyes. He dropped back to the floor, shook a stray pine needle from his hind foot, and ambled over to Maybelle. He meowed twice, but Maybelle was too focused on untying lights to notice. Not one to be deterred easily, the brown-and-black cat jumped onto the dining room table and sat down.

Maybelle drew back. "What's it doing?"

"He wants you to pet him," Kat said.

Maybelle didn't move. "It's staring at me."

"Tom's a he. And I've told you before he's an attention hog."

Maybelle regarded Tom. "It's bigger than I expected."

"He," Kat said, more firmly this time.

Tom reached a paw toward Maybelle's hand, prompting her to cringe.

"What's it doing now?" she asked.

"*He* wants you to pet him."

Maybelle clutched the lights to her chest. "Can you move it? I don't want to get fur on this outfit."

Kat frowned. Her mother didn't want to get fur on her outfit? Why had she worn it then? She knew she was going to be bunking with cats for three days.

Andrew, who must have returned at some point during their conversation, cleared his throat. "Mind if I put Tom in the bedroom with

Matty?" he asked.

"Oh, please," Maybelle said, visibly relaxing. "You're a lifesaver."

Andrew lifted Tom off of the table. The big cat didn't protest, clearly enjoying the human contact. To make up for Maybelle's dismissal, Kat gave him a pat as Andrew toted him past her.

Maybelle shook out the cord of lights and stepped back into the living room. "Now that those animals are out of the way, we can decorate."

Kat joined her by the tree. "I thought you liked cats."

"Whatever gave you that idea?"

"You never mentioned not liking them all those times I brought them up on our calls."

"Oh, well. You never asked, did you?"

"No." Kat didn't think she had to ask. After all, what kind of person didn't like cats?

Maybelle started stringing lights. "Give me a hand here, will you, Katherine?"

Kat grabbed one end of the cord. "I prefer Kat."

Maybelle's hands stopped moving. "What?"

"My name. I prefer Kat instead of Katherine."

"I've always called you Katherine."

"I know."

Maybelle raised one shoulder. "Okay, then. Kat it is."

Kat ground her molars together. She knew it was childish, but she had wanted her request to be met with more resistance. She wanted her mother to feel the same sense of betrayal about Kat never mentioning her preferred nickname that Kat did upon discovering that Maybelle had kept her dislike of cats a secret.

They worked in silence. Andrew must have decided he needed a break from Maybelle because he didn't reenter the room until the lights were up and they'd moved on to hanging baubles.

"Andrew," Maybelle said, beaming when she saw him. "Be a doll and help us reach some of those high branches, will you?"

"Sure thing, Ms. Harper."

"Please, call me Maybelle."

Before Andrew could acknowledge her request, there was a knock on the door. He looked at Kat. She lifted one shoulder.

Maybelle's face brightened. "Maybe that's Stephanie."

"Who's Stephanie?" Kat asked.

Maybelle dashed across the room, her heels not slowing her down one bit. "You know, my old friend."

But when she flung the door open, Larry, Kat's landlord and building manager, was standing there.

"Oh, hello." Maybelle leaned against the doorframe, one hip jutting out.

"Hi, Larry," Kat said, walking over to join them.

"Evening, Kat." The brawny, bald man's eyes flitted toward Maybelle, and a grin stretched across his face. "And if it ain't Maybelle Harper, in the flesh and blood."

Maybelle squinted at him. "Have we met?"

"Sure have. We went to Cherry Hills High together way back in the Dark Ages. You likely don't remember me."

Maybelle gasped. "Larry Carmichael?"

"Ah, you do remember."

"Of course I remember." Maybelle threw her arms around him. "You used to let me copy your math homework."

Larry chuckled. "Don't let Mrs. Bhatia hear you say that."

Maybelle pulled back and quirked her lips. "That old biddy can't still be alive."

"I wouldn't know. We lost touch after I passed algebra, though that took a good two years and one excruciatingly painful summer."

Maybelle giggled as if his words had turned her back into a schoolgirl.

Larry lifted up his hand, which Kat now saw held a box of candies. "I came up to give you this," he told Kat. "Somebody left it outside the front door."

"Aplets and Cotlets?" Kat said, recognizing the packaging.

"Oh, I love those things." Maybelle grabbed the box from Larry's hand.

Larry grinned. "I remember how you used to gobble these up. Who knows, if Kat's in the Christmas spirit she might let you have some."

"Are you sure it's for me?" Kat asked.

"Your name's on the card."

Sure enough, when Maybelle righted the box she could see 'K. Harper' scribbled on the envelope taped to the top.

"Thanks for bringing it up," Kat said.

"No problem," Larry replied. "I would've paid you a visit sooner if I had known your mom was here."

Maybelle swung the door open. "Would you like to come in and chat with us?"

"Nah." Larry took a step toward the elevator. "If I wanna take Christmas Eve off, I've got a few more chores to finish up tonight. This building doesn't maintain itself, I can tell you that."

Maybelle eyed him up and down. "I suppose it's not easy for a man as muscular as you to get a day off. It must be hard to find somebody who can fill your shoes."

Kat groaned, but Larry chortled so loudly she doubted anyone heard her.

"Ah, Maybelle, you always were a charmer." Larry affected a swagger Kat had never seen before as he retreated down the corridor. "You gals enjoy your evening."

Maybelle waved with a flamboyance that seemed unnecessary in Kat's opinion. "You, too."

Kat shut the door, and they rejoined Andrew.

"Somebody sent me this," Kat told him, taking the box from Maybelle.

"Who's it from?" he asked.

"I'm about to find out." Kat peeled the card off and ripped the envelope open. She read the words written inside aloud. " 'For the Aplet of my eye, I Cotlet resist giving you something sweet.' "

Maybelle laughed and clapped her hands. "I love it. How romantic."

Kat flipped the card over, then checked the envelope one more time. "There's no signature."

Maybelle's eyes bugged out. "Ooh, my daughter has a secret admirer!"

Kat and Andrew exchanged glances. Somehow, nothing about this Christmas was turning out as Kat had expected.

CHAPTER THREE

The next morning was Christmas Eve. When Kat awoke, Maybelle was already up and about. She knew because the bathroom door was closed, and her bladder was on the verge of bursting.

I can wait two minutes, Kat thought as she retreated to her bedroom. *The key is to focus on other things.*

Matty and Tom were relaxing on the bed. At Maybelle's request, the animals had been confined to the bedroom all night. Maybelle had been so vehement about not having any creatures sneak up on her while she was sleeping that Kat had to wonder if she thought Matty and Tom were waiting for a good opportunity to smother her. After the way Maybelle had talked to them yesterday, Kat wouldn't blame them.

Kat sat down on the mattress and rubbed Matty's head. "I shouldn't be so hard on her. Maybe she has a good reason for not liking cats. Maybe one really did try to suffocate her once."

Matty stretched her jaws into a yawn as though to communicate how tired she was of Maybelle Harper.

"Well, you'd better get used to her," Kat said. "She's here until Saturday, the day after Christmas."

That advice could apply to her too, Kat decided. Today she was going to focus on turning their relationship around. So what if their reunion had gotten off to a rocky start? Now that she'd had time to think about it, what had she really expected? She and her mother were seeing each other for the first time in over two decades. It was only natural they might not click right away.

Tom meowed and crept closer to Kat.

"I know it was love at first sight with us, Tom, but it's easier with you. We don't have a history."

While Kat petted the animals, she kept one ear out for the bathroom door opening. The building's poor insulation allowed her to hear her mother putzing around, the water running on full blast every few seconds.

"What is she doing?" Kat muttered. She looked at her alarm clock, noting that ten minutes had gone by since she'd first checked on the bathroom's availability. "Didn't it ever occur to her that I might need to get in there?"

Maybe not, Kat thought, opting to give her mother the benefit of the doubt. Maybelle lived alone, just like Kat. She probably wasn't used to sharing a bathroom.

At least there was an easy remedy for that. Kat nudged Tom aside and headed back to the bathroom. This time, she knocked.

"Who is it?" Maybelle trilled.

"Kat. I was wondering how much longer you'll be."

"Not much. I just started putting on my makeup."

Just started? What had she been doing for the last ten minutes then?

"What are our plans for breakfast?" Maybelle asked.

"I picked up bagels, coffee, and juice at the store yesterday."

"Huh. What about going out to eat?"

"Oh." Kat had hoped to get to know her mother a little better during a quiet breakfast at home. But maybe she didn't like bagels. "I guess we could go to Jessie's."

"Jessie's? You mean Jessie's Diner?" The door inched open, and Maybelle poked her head out. "I used to go there with my friends all the time."

"You did?" Maybe this would be the moment when they finally progressed from talking about the weather to sharing stories about their lives.

Maybelle grinned. "We loved it there."

"Who's 'we'?"

"Stephanie, Jonah, Quinn, and I. The four of us were thick as thieves back then."

"Yeah? What did you guys do?"

"Well, we had fun."

"I know that but—"

"Has their menu changed?" Maybelle interrupted.

Kat shrugged. "I don't remember everything they had back then. They still serve milkshakes though."

"Ugh." Maybelle made a face. "I can't drink milkshakes. They go straight to my thighs."

Kat couldn't stop her gaze from drifting to Maybelle's legs poking beneath the edge of the towel wrapped around her torso. She couldn't see what her mother was worried about.

"Give me another minute, and I'll be ready

to hit the road," Maybelle said before slamming the door shut.

Kat shifted her weight between her feet. She supposed she could hold her bladder for one more minute.

While she waited, she fed the cats. Then she got dressed. When Maybelle still hadn't emerged by the time Kat had her shoes on, a slow burn started to smolder in her chest.

"It's definitely been longer than a minute," she told Matty as the tortoiseshell ambled out of the kitchen.

Matty licked her lips, not appearing the least bit concerned over Kat's predicament. Now that she had a full belly, she wouldn't have any more use for her human until dinnertime.

When ten more minutes had passed, Kat had had enough.

She banged on the bathroom door. "Are you done yet?"

"Soon," Maybelle called back. "I just need to put on my makeup."

"You said you were doing that ten minutes ago!"

"I had to fix my hair first."

Kat stared at the door, her frustration building nearly to the bursting point. She had the wild urge to kick down the door and haul her mother out.

She took a deep breath, reminding herself to be reasonable. "I really have to go."

"Oh, well, in that case, just give me a minute."

Kat hopped around, counting down the seconds in her head. Closer to three minutes passed, but Maybelle finally swung the door open and sauntered out.

"Let me know when you're finished," she said. "I still need to do my makeup."

Kat managed a nod before racing into the bathroom. She completed her business in less than a minute but was tempted to linger just to stick it to her mother. Then she decided that would be juvenile.

"It's all yours," she told Maybelle as she opened the door.

When Maybelle finished putting on her makeup over an hour later, Kat was glad she'd interrupted when she had. There was no way she could have held her bladder for that long.

"My car's over there," Kat said after they stepped out of the apartment building.

"Why don't we take mine," Maybelle suggested. "I'm closer."

"Okay." Kat wanted to see how Maybelle managed to drive in her pumps anyway.

They climbed into Maybelle's sporty red coupe and headed out.

"Is there anything special you'd like to do today?" Kat asked. She had to admit that her mother was a pretty good driver. If she hadn't seen them herself, she would never know she had on three-inch heels. "My office is closed for Christmas Eve, so I'm free all day. We could drive around and look at the different house lights."

"Eh, I'm not really into that sort of thing."

Kat wasn't either, but she was struggling to think of something that might help to put them on better footing.

"You know what I'd really like?" Maybelle said.

"What's that?"

"To see Stephanie."

Kat's chest tightened. They'd only been in each other's company for half a day, and Maybelle was already itching to reconnect with her old friends? Was it too much to ask that she grant Kat more than a couple hours of uninterrupted mother-daughter time before she started seeking out the company of others?

Maybelle ran her palms along the steering wheel. "I gave Steph your address and told her to stop by when she has the chance. I had hoped she'd show up yesterday, but I guess she was too busy."

"You sound disappointed," Kat said, unable to hide the bite in her tone.

Maybelle didn't appear to notice. "You wouldn't believe what Steph and I used to get up to way back when," she said, a slight smile playing on her lips. "And when Quinn and Jonah joined us, nothing could stop us from tearing up the town."

"Yeah?" Kat twisted to face her better. "What did you guys get up to?"

"We would—" Maybelle cut herself off. "Eh, it was nothing. Just stuff you do when you're young."

Kat's heart sank. She had been looking forward to hearing about her mother's capers.

Unless the stories involved drugs, she considered. She knew her mother had struggled with addiction back then, and it wouldn't surprise her to learn that Maybelle had been high while she and her old cronies were having the time of their lives.

Maybelle frowned at the dashboard clock. "I can't believe Stephanie hasn't called yet."

"Maybe she wants to spend Christmas Eve with her family." *Unlike some other people in this car*, Kat silently added.

"I texted her while you were in the bathroom and asked if she was free for breakfast. She should have gotten back to me by now."

Kat folded her arms across her chest. "Yeah, it would be a shame if she couldn't make it."

"Hey." Maybelle glanced in her rearview mirror. "You see that truck back there?"

"What?"

"There's a silver truck a few car lengths behind us."

Kat rotated around to look out the back window. "The pickup?"

"Yeah. I think it's following me."

"Maybe it's your friend Stephanie."

Maybelle didn't notice the edge in Kat's voice. "Steph would never drive a truck. She's more of the Smart Car type."

"Then it could be somebody else on their way to Jessie's."

"Except that truck was tailing me yesterday, too."

A prickle of fear momentarily obscured Kat's irritation. "It followed you all the way from Oregon?"

"No. But when I pulled over to gas up at that service station on Culver Street, there was a truck just like it at one of the other pumps. And later, after I pulled onto your street, I noticed it behind me."

"Did you see the truck before you crossed into Cherry Hills?"

"No."

Kat relaxed. "So the driver lives here. This is a small town, remember? The odds of running into the same vehicle are pretty high. It's probably somebody out doing some last-minute Christmas shopping, and they're driving all over in search of the right gifts."

"Maybe," Maybelle said, but she didn't sound convinced.

Kat spotted their destination through the windshield. "If that truck is following you, we'll find out soon enough. Jessie's is coming up on the left."

Maybelle didn't say anything, but she did keep glancing in her rearview mirror.

Kat surveyed the restaurant's parking lot as they drew closer. She didn't know whether to blame Christmas Eve or the lull between breakfast and lunch for the lack of cars. Maybelle had spent so much time in the bathroom that they'd missed the morning rush.

"Hey." Kat swiveled her head around, watching as Jessie's receded in the driver's side window. "You missed the turn."

"I'm seeing if that truck follows us." Maybelle firmed her grip on the steering wheel. "I'm going to drive around for a while, see what it does."

"All right." Kat didn't figure this would take long. And if circling the block a couple times would help to put her mother's mind at ease, she would be a willing participant.

Maybelle took a right. Kat watched in the side mirror as the truck did the same. Maybelle turned a few more times, alternating between rights and lefts. When they ended up back at an intersection they'd already passed and the silver truck was still behind them, goosebumps broke out over Kat's skin.

"I should call Andrew," she said.

"So he can beat up the guy?" Maybelle asked.

"What? No. Andrew's a detective with the Cherry Hills Police Department."

Maybelle whistled. "Hunky and a cop."

"My point is, he'll know what to do about somebody following us around. He might even meet us somewhere and pull the driver over for questioning."

Maybelle straightened. "I don't need a man to save me."

"He's police. It's his job."

"One thing you're better off learning now,

Kat, is that relying on a man to get you through the tough times is only asking for trouble later."

Kat gritted her teeth. Her mother was choosing this moment to give her life advice, when their safety could be in jeopardy? And after all that flirting she'd done yesterday, Kat would have thought she'd jump on the excuse to see Andrew again.

"Besides," Maybelle went on, "I have a plan."

"What's that?"

"You and I are going to Jessie's just like we set off to do. Either this guy will take off, or we'll see who he is when he follows us into the restaurant."

Kat supposed it wasn't a terrible idea. Even if no customers were inside Jessie's Diner, at least a couple employees would be present. If the driver of the silver pickup meant them any harm, he wouldn't be able to do anything while they were there.

Maybelle turned at the next light and headed back toward the restaurant. Kat held her breath as they pulled into the parking lot. The silver pickup had stayed a ways back, and they had to wait a few seconds to see whether it would follow.

It didn't. The truck kept going, disappearing

down the road.

Kat exhaled. She didn't know who had been behind them, but evidently he didn't intend to reveal himself.

CHAPTER FOUR

"I didn't see that truck following us home," Kat commented when Maybelle pulled up to her apartment building.

Maybelle unbuckled her seat belt. "Me neither."

Their breakfast at Jessie's Diner had been tense. Or, at least it had been tense for Kat. Maybelle had been too busy texting Stephanie for Kat to get a sense as to whether she was worried about being followed. At any rate, Maybelle's preoccupation with her phone and Kat's constant glances through the restaurant windows in search of silver pickups had prevented them from engaging in any meaningful conversation. Kat was glad they were almost home.

She unlocked the front entrance and stepped into the building. While she was holding the door for her mother, she saw the postman standing by the bank of mailboxes on the far wall.

"Hi, Ron," she said.

Ron paused from sorting envelopes. "Morning, Kat."

"Why, hello there." Maybelle sashayed across the lobby. "You postal workers don't get Christmas Eve off?"

"No, ma'am."

Maybelle's lower lip jutted out. "That's atrocious."

After witnessing how Maybelle had acted around Andrew and Larry, Kat knew she shouldn't be surprised by her coquettish behavior, but somehow she never would have pegged Ron as her type. With pale, almost translucent skin, the tall man was thin to the point of being sickly.

"You know what I ought to do?" Maybelle said, setting one hand on her hip.

"What's that?" Ron asked.

"I ought to write my senators and tell them it's just shameful the way they work you civil servants to death. If anybody deserves a day off, it's you folks. Delivering mail through rain, sleet, and snow is bad enough."

Kat sighed. "Maybelle, why don't we go upstairs and let Ron do his job?"

Maybelle pivoted around to face her. "That's my whole point. He shouldn't have to do his job on the day before Christmas."

"I'm all right, ma'am," Ron said. "I'll be off tomorrow."

"I should hope so!" Maybelle replied. "Tomorrow's Christmas."

Kat took a step toward the elevator. "Let's go, Maybelle."

"Oh, Kat, you might want to take that with you." Ron pointed to a thin, rectangular box on the floor.

"What is it?" Maybelle bent down, presumably to inspect the package although Kat wasn't one hundred percent positive she wasn't simply offering Ron a better view of her cleavage.

"Dunno," Ron replied, his attention on the envelopes in his hand.

"Are you expecting anything?" Maybelle asked Kat.

She shook her head. "I ordered a . . ." She trailed off, deciding her mother wouldn't appreciate the gift she had purchased for Matty and Tom. "I ordered something, but I missed the deadline to have it shipped before Christmas."

Maybelle twisted around to study the package from another angle. "Maybe it came early."

"That box is too small to be what I'm expecting."

"It was here when I got here," Ron piped up. "There's no shipping label on it, just your name, Kat."

Creeping closer, Kat saw he was right. 'K. Harper' was scrawled across the top, but both her address and a return address were conspicuously absent.

Her skin tingled. Whoever had left this had to have been inside her building.

"I wonder what it is," Maybelle said, reaching for it.

"Wait!" Kat shouted.

The force of her exclamation sent Maybelle jumping back. Ron fell against the mailboxes, the envelopes in his hand scattering across the floor as his fingers flew to his throat.

Kat took a deep breath to calm her nerves. "I'm not sure we should touch it. It could be something dangerous."

"Like what?" Maybelle asked.

"I don't know. A bomb, maybe."

"A bomb?" Ron screeched.

Maybelle's eyes brightened. "I bet it's from your secret admirer, the one who sent you those Aplets and Cotlets." Before Kat could stop her, Maybelle picked up the box. "It's light." She held it up to her ear and gave it a shake. "Sounds like clothing."

Ron relaxed, but Kat didn't. She hoped it wasn't lingerie.

Maybelle hugged the package to her chest. "Come on. We'll open this upstairs."

"Or, we could throw it away," Kat suggested.

"Now you're just being silly." Maybelle flashed Ron a smile over her shoulder. "You have yourself a Merry Christmas."

"You, too," Ron replied before crouching down to gather up the dropped envelopes.

Kat and Maybelle didn't speak as they took the elevator up to the third floor. The anxiety Kat had felt all throughout breakfast was back. As she walked down the corridor to her unit, she kept darting uneasy glances at the box in Maybelle's hands.

Both Matty and Tom were lounging under the Christmas tree when the humans entered the apartment. The minute they saw Maybelle their eyes grew big and they sprang to their feet. Staying low to the ground as if that would prevent the enemy from detecting them, they scampered off to the bedroom.

Maybelle slid the box on the coffee table,

kicked off her heels, and took a seat on the sofa. "Open it," she said to Kat, practically bouncing up and down.

Kat sat next to her mother, but she didn't reach for the box. "I should call Andrew first."

"Oh, now. You're not still stuck on that crazy bomb notion, are you?"

Given that the package had yet to explode, Kat was no longer concerned about a bomb. Still, opening a secret admirer's gift without Andrew around felt tantamount to cheating on him.

Maybelle grabbed the box and dropped it in Kat's lap before shoving her hand into her purse. "I've got a nail file in here you can use to cut through that tape."

Kat sighed. Her mother obviously wasn't going to give up.

Taking the nail file, Kat held her breath as she severed the tape. When she was able to lift the lid away from the box, a mass of tissue paper burst free.

Maybelle stuck her head closer, flooding Kat's nasal cavity with her perfume. "What is it?" she asked.

Kat folded the tissue paper down. "Some pink fabric with flower blossoms on it." She pulled it out and placed the box on the floor.

Maybelle snatched the fabric from Kat's hands. "It's a pashmina."

Matty and Tom must have decided they didn't dislike Maybelle enough for her to keep them away from a new box and a sea of tissue paper. They emerged from the hallway, making a beeline for the discarded gift packaging.

Maybelle pulled her legs up to her chest. "What are they doing?"

"Playing."

Maybelle watched as Tom marched across the paper and Matty climbed into the box. "I thought they were charging at me. That big one looked like it was going to attack."

If you keep calling him an 'it,' he just might, Kat thought.

Matty's weight proved to be too much for the box. The sides collapsed underneath her. Undeterred, the tortoiseshell dug her claws into the bottom, turning it into a makeshift cat scratcher. Meanwhile, Tom had his head stuck under a section of tissue paper. After looking around, he shook the paper aside, exposing a cream-colored envelope.

Kat's breakfast congealed in her stomach. "Look, another card."

"What does it say?" Maybelle asked as she set her feet back on the floor.

Kat picked up the envelope and pulled out the card, reading the words aloud. " 'Seeing you is like spotting a spring blossom in the winter, something to keep me warm during the long, cold nights.' "

Maybelle clasped her hands together. "Oh, that's delightful."

"Don't you mean disturbing?" Kat said, tossing the card onto the coffee table.

"For someone who was worried about receiving a bomb, you don't seem very happy."

"I'll admit this is a smidgen better than a bomb."

Maybelle grinned and held up the pashmina. "So, what are you going to do with this?"

"Give it to Andrew," Kat replied.

Maybelle looked appalled. "You can't give your boyfriend a pashmina for Christmas! This is for girls."

"That's not what I meant. There might be evidence on it."

"Evidence? Evidence of what?"

"You know, fingerprints or microfibers, something that will tell us who left it here."

"You mean hunt down your secret admirer?" Maybelle frowned. "But that would ruin the fun."

Kat decided not to tell her this was only fun

for one of them.

Maybelle yanked her purse into her lap and started rummaging through it. "I've got to text Stephanie. She'll love this."

Still bothered by the reality of having a secret admirer, Kat barely felt even the slightest blip of jealousy when her mother proceeded to pull out her cell phone and once again ignored her in favor of texting Stephanie.

CHAPTER FIVE

Kat felt guilty for fleeing the apartment without inviting her mother along, but she needed a break. The way Maybelle had kept going on and on about Kat's secret admirer made her want to scream. When Maybelle had actually draped the pashmina around her shoulders and proceeded to prance around the living room, she knew she had to get out of there.

Besides, it wasn't as if she were going to stay out all day. She just needed an hour or so for herself. Matty and Tom would never forgive her if she left them alone with Maybelle for longer than that.

Kat drove aimlessly, her heart heavy. She had pictured this visit unfolding so differently. Was it possible too much damage had been done to her and Maybelle's relationship to ever repair it? When she was growing up, she used to be envious of the foster kids who saw their parents regularly, even when they came home from visitation days spewing complaints. If she had fully understood what her own mother was like back then, maybe she would have been more sympathetic.

Kat played through the few childhood memories she had of Maybelle. Try as she might, she couldn't remember all the flirting, makeup, and exuberance. Had she suppressed everything, or could a person really change that much in twenty years?

The Cherry Hills Police Department appeared up ahead. Although she hadn't left the apartment with any particular destination in mind, she made a quick decision and veered into the parking lot. She wanted to tell Andrew about her newest anonymous gift anyway.

"Hey, Kat," the officer manning the front desk said when she walked into the station. "You here for Andrew?"

"Yeah, is he in?"

"Sure is." He nodded toward the door that led to the inner office. "Head on back if you'd like."

Kat crossed the lobby. "Thanks."

"Happy holidays."

"You, too."

The door to Andrew's too-small office was open. She knocked once to announce her presence. "You accepting visitors?"

Andrew tore his eyes away from the computer monitor, a grin forcing his dimples out. "For you? Always."

Kat worked her way into the lone visitor chair, angling her legs so her knees weren't pressed against the front of the desk. "Sorry to barge in on you like this, but I needed a break from Maybelle."

Andrew chuckled. "She can't be that bad."

"She's worse."

"Give it time. It might take a while before you're comfortable around each other."

"Well, if it doesn't happen soon, it probably won't ever happen." The reality of her statement sparked an ache in Kat's heart. "Tomorrow's Christmas, and the next day she heads back to Estacada."

"You realize you actually have to spend time with her if you want your relationship to improve, right?"

"I have spent time with her. All of yesterday evening and this morning."

"That's less than twenty-four hours," Andrew said. "That's hardly long enough to make up for the twenty years you were apart."

"You're right, I know." Kat sighed. "I just thought this would be easier. I mean, we get along fine on the phone. I don't understand how she can be so different in person."

"Your phone conversations last for five minutes, during which you talk about the weather and what Matty and Tom did that week."

"That's another thing." Kat sat up, feeling a burst of indignation. "Before yesterday she never once mentioned she hates cats."

"I don't think she *hates* them," Andrew hedged.

"Oh, she hates them. Didn't you hear how she kept calling Tom an 'it'?"

"I doubt her intent was—"

"You know what really bugs me?" Kat interrupted, all of her pent-up frustration bubbling to the surface. "She lets me go on and on about the cats during our calls. And she laughs when I talk about them. She *laughs*. Then she gets here and acts like Matty and Tom are the devil incarnate. Was she even listening to what I was saying all those times on the phone, or was she just pretending?"

"I'm sure she—"

"And I'll tell you another thing. I'm getting

awfully tired of hearing about Stephanie. You'd think she only came back to Cherry Hills to see her old friend. In fact, if I hear that name one more time, I swear I'm going to lose it."

Andrew gave her a soft smile. "Sorry things aren't going better for you."

"Me, too." She sagged against the back of the chair. "Between putting up with Maybelle and getting another gift from this secret admirer, this is shaping up to be the worst Christmas ever."

Andrew stilled. "You got another gift?"

Kat nodded. "A pashmina."

"A pashmina?"

"It's like a shawl. The box it came in was sitting by the mailboxes when Maybelle and I got home from breakfast. Whoever this person is, he had to have delivered it himself. It wasn't postmarked, and my address wasn't printed anywhere."

Andrew half rose from his chair. "This guy was in your building?"

Kat lifted one shoulder. "Either that or he left the package outside the door and Larry or someone brought it in."

Andrew didn't reply, but Kat could tell from the set of his jaw that he wasn't happy. He would probably like what she had to say next even less.

"There's something else you should know," she began.

Andrew sank back into his chair, his hands balling into fists as they landed on the desk. "What's that?"

"A silver truck followed my mother and me around this morning."

"You get a license plate number?"

She shook her head.

"Can you describe the driver?" Andrew asked.

"He stayed too far back. But Maybelle said she saw the same truck yesterday."

"So Maybelle was the one being followed, not you?"

Kat frowned. "I'm not sure. Do you think he's the person who's been leaving me gifts?"

"Not necessarily. But we can't rule it out either."

Kat straightened, something clicking in her brain. "Now that I think about it, neither one of those gifts had my first name on them. They just had the initial K. What if they weren't meant for me?"

"Who else would they be for?"

"Maybelle."

"Then they would have been addressed to

M. Harper."

"K could stand for Kelly, the name she goes by down in Oregon."

Andrew's forehead furrowed. "But doesn't she also go by a different last name there?"

"Watson," Kat confirmed. "But this secret admirer might not know that. If he followed her to my place yesterday, he could have looked at the names on the buzzer, seen that a K. Harper lived there, and assumed it was her. I don't think anybody else in the building has the same first initial as me."

They stared at each other, unease swirling in Kat's stomach. She pictured her mother throwing that pashmina over her shoulder and running her hands over the box of Aplets and Cotlets, pure joy stamped on her face.

"She liked the gifts," Kat murmured.

"What?" Andrew said.

"Maybelle liked both of the gifts this guy left for her. No, scratch that. She *loved* them. It's almost like her secret admirer is familiar with her tastes."

"That would suggest she knows him."

A chill made its way down Kat's spine. "Either that or he's been following her around for a lot longer than a day."

CHAPTER SIX

Maybelle was sitting on the couch staring at her phone when Andrew and Kat walked into the apartment. She had plugged in the Christmas tree lights, and Kat had to admit the effect of all those twinkling red and white lights made the place seem more festive.

It was too bad Kat's mood was anything but.

Maybelle looked up from her phone. "Kat, you're home. And you brought your stud."

"His name is Andrew," Kat said, shutting the door a little too hard.

"I know what his name is." Maybelle winked at Andrew.

Kat sat down on the couch opposite her mother. Matty jumped into her lap and gave her a look that Kat interpreted as the feline equivalent of a glare. Clearly the tortoiseshell hadn't appreciated being left alone with their anti-cat houseguest.

Kat rubbed Matty's ears, hoping there were no hard feelings. "Maybelle," she began, "I was talking to Andrew about the pashmina and the candies."

"Aren't they wonderful?" Maybelle asked Andrew.

"No," Kat interjected. "They're not wonderful at all."

Maybelle jerked back, and Kat realized she might have spoken more forcefully than she'd intended.

Andrew took a seat next to Kat. "Maybelle, we have some serious concerns about the items that have shown up here recently. For one thing, we have reason to believe they were meant for you and not Kat."

Tom, who had been hunched in the box the pashmina had come in, lifted his head. A second later he scrambled to his feet and tiptoed away from the packaging, almost as if he wanted nothing to do with anything meant for Maybelle Harper.

"The items were addressed to K. Harper, but we were thinking the K could stand for Kelly instead of Kat," Kat said.

"You mean this is mine?" Maybelle swiped the pashmina off of the coffee table and held it against her cheek.

"No," Kat said. "I mean, yes, it was meant for you, but you can't keep it."

"Why not?"

"Because it's from somebody who could be dangerous. By accepting his gifts you're encouraging him, and his behavior may escalate."

Tom turned toward Maybelle and meowed, as though to drive home Kat's point.

Andrew cleared his throat. "Maybelle, have you received anonymous presents in the past?"

She shook her head. "This is a first."

"Whoever sent you these items appears to have an idea of what type of things you like," Andrew said. "That suggests you might know each other."

Tom leapt onto the loveseat next to Maybelle and sniffed the pashmina as though he were attempting to identify the gift giver by scent.

"Have you broken up with anybody recently?" Andrew asked.

Maybelle pushed Tom aside. "I never would have broken up with a man who gave me stuff as nice as this."

Not even if he had a cat? Kat wondered as

Tom stalked off and took refuge under the tree.

"Can you think of anybody who might be behind these gifts?" Andrew said. "Perhaps a friend has been pushing you to take things to the next level and you've been rejecting his advances."

Maybelle winked. "I'll tell you right now, if I had a male friend with such good taste, I wouldn't be rejecting anything from him."

Kat could feel her blood pressure rising. Didn't her mother realize how serious this was? She was talking as though having a man secretly pining for her was a joke or an opportunity to receive free stuff.

Maybelle ran her palms over the pashmina. "Feel this fabric. Have you ever laid your hands on anything so silky soft?"

"You shouldn't be touching that," Kat snapped.

"Why not?"

Kat was on the verge of exploding. "Because it's from a deranged stalker!"

Matty flattened her ears back. Evidently deciding that Kat was the deranged one, the tortoiseshell stood up, crept across Andrew's legs, and relocated to the other side of the sofa.

Kat jumped off the couch and snatched the pashmina out of Maybelle's hands. Then she plucked the box of Aplets and Cotlets and the two cards off of the coffee table and dumped everything into Andrew's lap. "Andrew's going to see if he can get any fingerprints off of this stuff."

Maybelle slouched in her seat. She looked like a kid whose Christmas gifts had been taken away.

"Kat told me a silver truck was following you yesterday and again this morning," Andrew said.

Maybelle lifted her eyes up to meet his. "That's right."

"Can you tell me anything about it? Did you see the driver, or happen to catch his license plate number?"

Maybelle shook her head. "But I'm sure he doesn't mean any harm. He's probably just somebody with a little crush. Men are always buzzing around me."

"Who are these men exactly?" Andrew asked. "Names would be helpful."

"You can't expect me to list all of them." Maybelle looked shocked by the request.

Kat dropped back onto the couch and crossed her arms over her chest. "You know, if you weren't such a tease you might not be in this mess."

"What do you mean?" Maybelle said.

"You're a relentless flirt," Kat bit out. "Is it any wonder you attracted the wrong man's attention?"

Andrew set his palm on Kat's knee. "Assigning blame isn't our goal here."

Kat pushed his hand away. "She even hit on you, so don't deny she shouldn't tone it down."

The buzzer sounded. Kat stiffened, her anger morphing into fear. She prayed whoever was here hadn't come to drop off another present.

The irony didn't escape her. She imagined they were the only people in Cherry Hills dreading the appearance of more gifts this Christmas.

CHAPTER SEVEN

Maybelle was the first to react. "Maybe that's Stephanie," she said, jumping up and running toward the buzzer.

Andrew glanced at Kat. She figured he remembered her complaints at the police station and was waiting to see if this was the reference to Maybelle's friend that finally sent her over the edge.

But Kat had bigger concerns now than vying with Stephanie for her mother's attention. Even if Maybelle wasn't bothered by an unknown man following her around Cherry Hills, Kat was.

"Stephanie!" Maybelle screeched into the buzzer. "Come on up!"

Although Kat was somewhat relieved their

caller wasn't the secret admirer, Maybelle's announcement didn't bring her much joy. Stephanie wasn't far behind Maybelle's stalker on the list of people she least wanted to see.

Maybelle threw open the front door and hovered in the doorway. "I wonder if she looks the same as she did twenty years ago," she said, fluffing her hair. "Steph was always a bombshell."

Kat didn't respond. From the way Maybelle had her gaze trained in the direction of the elevator, she figured her mother was talking more to herself anyway.

Kat caught Tom's eye across the room. When she held out her hand and rubbed her fingertips together, the feline stood up and ambled over.

"Maybelle Harper!"

The shrill squeal caused Tom to flatten his ears back.

"Oh my word!" Maybelle shrieked. "It's really you!"

Kat rolled her eyes at Andrew as she listened to Maybelle and Stephanie enthusing over their reunion. But as annoyed as she was, she was more hurt than anything. Her mother hadn't acted nearly as emotional upon seeing Kat yesterday.

The door shut, and the two women walked into the living room. Kat pulled Tom into her lap as she surreptitiously eyed her mother's old friend. After hearing her described as a bombshell, she had expected to see someone as glamorous as Maybelle, but Stephanie looked more like a plump, matronly housewife. Her brown hair had streaks of gray running through it, and she was dressed in a simple sweatsuit and sneakers.

"Stephanie, this is my daughter, Kat," Maybelle said, a huge grin on her face. "Didn't she turn into a gorgeous young woman?"

Stephanie regarded Kat with something bordering on affection. "She did indeed." Her gaze drifted toward Tom. "And that cat of yours is just darling. Look at his rich markings and those expressive green eyes."

Despite her dislike of Stephanie on principle, Kat could feel some of her animosity dissipating. "This is Tom."

"Tom, like Tom Cat." Stephanie laughed, and Kat couldn't help but notice she had a nice laugh. "Cute."

"Matty, Matilda, is on the other end of the couch there." Kat pointed to the tortoiseshell, buoyed by the presence of another cat person. "She's kind of aloof, but she's friendly."

Stephanie walked over to Matty and rubbed her between the ears. "Hey there, sweetheart."

Matty closed her eyes and pressed her head into Stephanie's hand. Kat could hear the tortoiseshell purring, and her opinion of Stephanie ratcheted up another notch.

"Enough about that." Maybelle grabbed Stephanie's elbow and led her over to the loveseat. "We have so much to catch up on."

Kat felt a flash of irritation. Would it really kill Maybelle to let Stephanie pet Matty for one minute?

Maybelle set her hand on Stephanie's. "Remember that text I sent you about Kat's secret admirer?"

"Yes."

"Well, it turns out he's actually my secret admirer."

"You don't say." Stephanie hunched closer to Maybelle. "Who is he?"

"I don't know, but he has the best taste in gifts."

"He's a psycho," Kat interjected.

Stephanie twisted toward Kat, a frown pulling at her lips. "He is?"

"No," Maybelle said, just as Kat said, "Yes."

Kat glared at her mother, then turned to address Stephanie. "He's been stalking her ever since she came back to Cherry Hills, and he's sent over two presents already."

Stephanie eyed Maybelle. "He sounds obsessed."

"Oh." Maybelle dismissed her concern with a flick of her wrist. "He's probably just shy."

Kat's anger flared. She was about to stress the importance of taking this seriously when Andrew put his hand on her knee.

"Let her enjoy her visit," he whispered.

"Why?" Kat challenged, spoiling for a fight. "I'm not enjoying mine."

Maybelle rotated toward Stephanie, oblivious to Kat's increasingly foul mood. "So, tell me what the old gang is up to. Whatever happened to Jonah?"

Stephanie grinned. "I married him."

Maybelle gasped. "You did not."

"I did." Stephanie paused, her smile fading. "Then we divorced five years later. He still lives in town, but we don't speak."

Maybelle smirked. "Oh, it was one of *those* divorces."

"It was bound to fail. We wed for all the wrong reasons."

"I was hoping we could all hang out again, too."

"Yeah, because why waste time with me

when she could be out with her friends?" Kat hissed at Andrew.

He didn't respond, which was probably for the best. Kat knew she was being unreasonable, but this whole situation had thrust her back to the 1990s, when she was a lonely kid longing for a piece of her mother's attention.

"Remember when you, me, and Jonah went up to Wenatchee that one spring?" Maybelle said.

Stephanie cocked her head. "For the Apple Blossom Festival?"

Maybelle nodded. "We were so bummed Quinn couldn't make it, but we still had the best time."

Stephanie chuckled. "We were terrible back then, weren't we? I remember swiping food from a few of the vendors when they weren't looking."

Maybelle's eyes twinkled with mischief. "And that old crone selling corn on the cob bopped Jonah over the head with one of the ears. Remember that? Butter was dripping from his hair the rest of the day."

Maybe having Stephanie here wasn't so bad after all, Kat considered. Her mother seemed more willing to share stories of her past with her friend around.

"What about Quinn?" Maybelle asked. "You still keep in touch with him?"

Stephanie shook her head. "He moved to Seattle. His family's still here, so I see them around town, but other than the occasional hello we don't speak."

Maybelle's face fell. "That's too bad. The four of us used to be so close."

Stephanie shrugged. "Things change."

Maybelle squeezed Stephanie's leg. "At least you're still the same."

"Oh, come on now. I'm a dowdy middle-aged frump." Stephanie scrutinized Maybelle. "But you look fab. What have you been using on your skin?"

"I have a whole ritual. First thing in the morning, I . . ."

Kat tuned out as Maybelle launched into a description of her beauty routine. If talking about it took as long as doing it, she didn't think they would be changing topics anytime soon.

Matty apparently had no interest in Maybelle's skin-care regimen either. She hopped onto the floor and padded over to the tree. After examining a nearby bauble, she swatted at it until it tumbled to the carpet.

Tom's head shot up. He looked astonished to learn that the ornaments weren't actually anchored to the tree. Unable to resist seeing for himself, he scrambled off of Kat's lap, and pretty soon both cats were well on their way to stripping the tree of all its decorations.

Maybelle stopped talking when one of the baubles rolled in her direction. "They're making a mess."

"They're having fun," Kat said, jumping to Matty and Tom's defense.

"It's not every day they have a tree inside the house," Stephanie said. "Who can blame them for being excited? And, Katherine, I think your cats are darling."

"Thank you." The words came out flat. As nice a person as Stephanie seemed to be, Kat still wished she would head on home and give Kat her mother back.

Maybelle pulled her feet onto the loveseat and tucked them underneath her. "Now, where was I?"

"You were telling me about that moisturizer that takes ten years off," Stephanie replied.

"Oh, right. So, every night . . ."

Kat studied Maybelle. As annoying as her bathroom takeover had been this morning, she had to admit she did have nice skin. It was no wonder men flocked to her.

Kat recalled the way Larry's face had brightened when Maybelle had answered the door. She couldn't remember Larry ever mentioning a wife or girlfriend. He didn't wear a wedding ring that she could recall, although that might merely be because he worked with his hands all day.

Kat's heart started beating faster as something else occurred to her. Larry had shown up at Kat's apartment soon after Maybelle had arrived. In fact, he had been the one to find that box of Aplets and Cotlets outside the building. At least, he'd claimed he'd found it. Now, she wasn't so sure.

"Andrew," Kat said, tugging on his sleeve, "do you think Larry might be Maybelle's secret admirer?"

"Larry your landlord?" Andrew asked.

She nodded. "They have a history together, and you saw how he responded when she answered the door yesterday. Plus, he has free access to the building. He could have left that pashmina downstairs, realizing it would look fishy if he 'found' both of her secret admirer's gifts."

Andrew rubbed his chin, seeming to ponder that.

"And Larry's always lugging tools and materials around to fix one thing or another," Kat went on, warming to her theory. "I've never paid attention to what he drives, but don't a lot of handymen prefer pickups?"

"I'll look up what vehicles are registered in his name when I'm back at the station," Andrew said.

"Well, what are you waiting for?" Kat stood up and shooed him toward the door.

Andrew grinned. "Eager to get rid of me now that I have a purpose, huh?"

"More like, I'd sleep a lot better tonight if I knew Maybelle's secret admirer was somebody like Larry." Kat liked Larry, and he had always treated her with respect. If he was the person behind the gifts, she was pretty sure he hadn't sent them over with any nefarious intent.

If Larry wasn't the guilty party, well, then someone a lot more dangerous could still be lurking out there.

Andrew gathered up Maybelle's gifts, and Kat walked him to the door. After a quick peek to make sure Maybelle and Stephanie were still engrossed in conversation, she set her hands on Andrew's shoulders and tipped her face up to give him a peck on the lips.

"Call me when you know what Larry drives," she said.

"Will do." He adjusted the items in his arms.

"I'll let you know if I get anything off of this stuff, too."

"Thanks," she said, feeling a little less anxious than she had been a minute ago.

But her comfort didn't last long. As soon as she shut the door, both Maybelle and Stephanie dissolved into peals of laughter.

Steeling herself, she went to rejoin the reunion.

CHAPTER EIGHT

"That was nice, don't you think?" Maybelle said after seeing Stephanie to the door.

Kat looked over at her from her spot on the couch. "What was?"

Maybelle resettled on the loveseat. "Our visit with Stephanie."

"*Our* visit? She barely said two words to me."

"Oh, now, that's not true. She told you what nice cats you have. And weren't you happy to see her again?"

Kat rubbed her temple. Stephanie's visit had left her with a tiny headache in addition to a boatload of resentment. "This is the first time we've met," she said.

Matty and Tom had grown tired of knocking baubles around a half hour ago. Tom was now roosting on the crushed pashmina box, and Matty was watching Maybelle through drooping eyelids as she rested underneath the tree. So far, the animals seemed to be enjoying this Christmas a lot more than Kat.

Maybelle sat up. "You don't remember?"

"Remember what?"

"Stephanie used to watch you when you were a baby."

Kat folded her arms across her chest. "I hate to break this to you, but I don't remember being a baby."

"Well, she used to care for you when I was working, up until you were two and they—" Maybelle choked on the last word. She took a moment to compose herself, then said, "Up until Social Services took you away from me."

"And you expect me to remember that? I was two."

"But you both always had so much fun together. I thought you'd remember." Maybelle worked a wrinkle in her pants. "I used to get so jealous watching the way you clung to her."

Kat snorted. "Yeah, it must have been tough when Stephanie couldn't hang out because I was being such a selfish, needy baby."

Maybelle's head jerked up. "I was jealous because you liked her so much more than you liked me."

"What did you expect when you dumped me with her to . . . work did you say? Or were you really off doing drugs?"

Maybelle's shoulders slumped. "I wasn't a very good mother to you, was I?"

"No, you weren't," Kat agreed.

"I didn't have my head on straight back then." Maybelle stared down at her lap as if she were afraid to look Kat in the eye. "But Stephanie, she was always so sure of herself. I knew she was good with you—she was good *to* you—so I often dropped you off with her when I didn't think I could take care of you myself."

Kat clamped her mouth shut. If her mother expected a thank-you for leaving her with someone else, she would have a long wait ahead of her.

Maybelle gave Kat a sad smile. "You never wanted to leave Steph. Whenever I'd come to pick you up, you'd cry and hold your arms out for her. She used to do this thing with you, where she'd sing you this song when it was time for you to go back home with me. The bye-bye song, was what she called it."

"I don't remember any songs."

"It went like this." Maybelle hummed a few notes that sounded eerily familiar. "It would get you to calm down—at least until we were alone again. Then you'd be inconsolable for hours."

Matty joined Kat on the couch. She settled in Kat's lap and began bathing herself.

"You called her mama first." Maybelle's eyes shone, as if she were holding back tears. "My heart cracked when she told me, but she thought it was funny. I think she was secretly pleased you preferred her to me."

Kat frowned. "I don't remember any of this."

"Like you said, you were probably too young." Maybelle lifted one shoulder. "But I thought some part of you would recognize Stephanie, even if you didn't have any solid memories of her. I thought you'd want to see her again."

"Wait a minute," Kat said, something occurring to her for the first time. "You invited Stephanie over for *me*?"

"Naturally, I wanted to see her too, but I thought you two would enjoy reconnecting."

Kat listed against the sofa. Now that she knew what an important role Stephanie had played in her early life, she wanted to invite her back so she could do their visit over, this time with her being a much more gracious hostess.

Kat's cell phone rang. She fished it out of her jeans pocket, half expecting to see Stephanie's name on the caller ID despite how she wasn't in her contact list. But it was Andrew.

"Hi," Kat answered.

"I looked up Larry Carmichael's vehicle registration," he said.

"And?"

"And he drives a pickup."

Kat's breath hitched.

"But it's a red Chevy," Andrew continued.

"Oh." Kat wasn't sure whether that was welcome news or not.

"I sent those gifts down to the lab," Andrew told her. "If you think of anybody else who might be the person we're looking for, give me a call. I'll be in my office for a few more hours yet."

"Okay. Thanks for this."

They disconnected, and Kat tossed her cell phone onto the coffee table.

"Who was that?" Maybelle asked.

"Andrew." She opted not to elaborate, loath to admit to suspecting Larry now that he had been cleared of any wrongdoing.

Maybelle touched her hair. "I like Andrew."

"I know." *I can tell by your shameless flirting*, Kat thought.

"You have much better taste in men than I did when I was your age."

"Yeah?"

Maybelle tilted her head back and stared at the ceiling. "Quinn, the guy me and Steph were talking about, was the epitome of my type way back when. He was the kind of guy who rode a motorcycle without a helmet and stayed out all night when he had to work the next morning. Dangerous and irresponsible."

Kat's interest piqued. Was her mother finally going to open up about her past?

"I wanted him to ask me out for the longest time." Maybelle worried her lower lip. "I guess he could tell I was more trouble than I was worth because he never did. It was probably for the best that we lost touch. He was bad news."

"Was he into drugs too?" Kat hadn't meant to blurt out the question, but it escaped before she could censor herself. Still, she didn't take it back. She and Maybelle had never talked about her drug history, and Kat was genuinely curious.

Maybelle nodded, lowering her gaze.

Kat's heart twisted at the anguished look on her mother's face. She stroked Matty's back, needing something calming to focus on. But Matty wasn't finished with her bath. She gave

Kat the stink eye, then furiously started re-licking the area that had been sullied.

Maybelle drew in a deep breath. "You know, I always hated Christmas."

Kat's head snapped in her direction. "You did?"

"It always killed me, being away from you while everybody else was celebrating with their families."

A lump lodged itself in Kat's throat. She was both surprised and sad to learn her mother had felt the same way she had all those years they were apart.

Maybelle fingered the edge of the couch cushion. "Kat, I don't believe I've ever apologized for not being there for you. I'm sorry I wasn't a better mother."

Kat swallowed hard. "At least you had enough sense to leave me with somebody who could take care of me."

"I'm sorry you don't remember Steph."

"Me too, but I'm glad I got to meet her tonight."

They fell silent, the lights of the tree sparkling on the far side of the room. Maybe this Christmas wouldn't turn out to be so bad after all, Kat thought, feeling hopeful for the first time that day.

That was assuming, of course, that Maybelle's stalker stayed far, far away.

CHAPTER NINE

Christmas Day dawned bright and sunny. Luckily, Kat managed to snag the bathroom before Maybelle holed up in there. Apparently she didn't even take holidays off from her skin-care routine. By the time they sat down to eat bagels, it was already noon.

Unlike their breakfast at Jessie's Diner the day before, this meal passed pleasantly. Maybelle left her cell phone in the living room, and Kat didn't have to worry about keeping watch for stalkers. Plus, Kat had felt something shift between them after she'd learned about Stephanie's role in her upbringing. The atmosphere between them was definitely less tense, at least.

The cats clearly sensed the change between the humans, too. Neither one seemed con-

cerned with Maybelle's presence as they wolfed
down their special serving of holiday wet food.
When everyone relocated to the living room,
Tom even jumped onto the empty couch cushion next to Maybelle. It was as though he had
completely forgotten about being rebuffed by
her earlier.

On the other sofa, Kat held her breath while
she waited to see how her mother would react.
Maybelle scooted to the end of the loveseat, but
she didn't shoo Tom away. Tom must have considered that to be an invitation to move closer.
He laid down, draping his front legs across
Maybelle's thigh.

Maybelle pulled her hands up to her chest.
"What does it want?"

"He wants you to pet him," Kat replied.

Maybelle didn't move.

"The easiest way to get rid of him is to give
in," Kat told her. "He's been known to bug
people for hours until he gets what he wants. If
you're lucky, he'll be content with a few pats
then wander somewhere else."

Tom's tail swept back and forth as he waited
for Maybelle to acknowledge him. Scrunching
up her nose, she inched one hand toward the cat
and brushed him with the tips of her fingers.

"He's soft," she said, her voice lilting in

surprise.

Kat didn't miss Tom's upgrade from an 'it' to a 'he,' and she considered her mother's choice of pronoun to be a minor victory. That minor victory turned into a major triumph when Maybelle actually began stroking Tom in earnest.

Tom flopped onto his side and stretched out.

Maybelle flinched. "What's he doing?"

"Getting comfortable. He likes having his belly rubbed."

Maybelle hesitated a moment, then gave Tom's stomach a tentative scratch. When he rolled onto his back, she grinned.

"I'm starting to see why you like this creature," she said. "My cat was always scratching and biting."

Kat's eyebrows migrated up her forehead. "You had a cat?"

"Once, when I was seven or eight, before it ran away. In fairness, I was pretty mean to it, too. I remember pulling its tail on more than a few occasions."

"Your parents didn't stop you?" Kat asked.

"No."

From Maybelle's terse response, Kat gathered that her mother didn't think much of her own parents. And as much as she wanted to hear about the grandparents she had never met, Kat didn't push the topic. Maybe bad parenting was a Harper family legacy that had been passed down for more generations than either one of them was comfortable discussing.

"What was it like growing up in foster care?" Maybelle asked.

"What?" Kat said, taken aback by the question.

Maybelle averted her eyes, focusing on Tom's belly rub. "I've always wondered if I did the right thing leaving you behind."

Her confession left Kat momentarily tongue-tied. It had never occurred to her that Maybelle might have as many unanswered questions about Kat's life as Kat did about hers.

Kat carefully considered how to respond. "It was lonely sometimes, but nobody mistreated me," she finally said. She wasn't ready to let Maybelle off the hook for abandoning her yet, but neither did she want her to wrongly conclude that she had been abused.

"It was lonely for me back then, too," Maybelle said. "With addiction, it's easy to find yourself isolated."

"Addiction is one thing. Being deserted when your mother skips town is something else entirely."

Maybelle nodded in what seemed like slow motion. "You're right. I guess I have a knack for letting down those I love—and leading on those I don't love."

Kat worked her jaw. "I shouldn't have blamed you for encouraging this stalker. You're the victim, not the culprit. I was upset and worried, and I took it out on you."

Maybelle rested her hand on Tom's side. "Thank you for saying that. And I hope you know you weren't the cause of your own circumstances either. That was completely my doing."

Kat rose from the couch, unsettled by where their conversation was headed. Although she appreciated her mother taking responsibility for her actions all those years ago, she still wasn't ready to forgive her.

"I'm going to make some hot chocolate," she said, needing a moment alone to get her emotions in check. "Would you like some?"

Maybelle shook her head. "That would go straight to my thighs. I'll take some more of that coffee though. It was pretty good for instant."

Kat went to fetch their beverages. When she returned to the living room, Tom was snuggled against Maybelle's leg and Maybelle had her cell phone out.

"Checking in with Stephanie?" Kat asked, handing Maybelle her coffee and reclaiming her seat on the sofa.

"Just seeing what the weather's supposed to be like tomorrow. I'm hoping it doesn't snow during my drive back."

"Oh." Reminded that their time together was almost over, Kat felt an unexpected sense of loss.

"Hey." Maybelle set her phone in her lap. "Now would be a good time for you to open your Christmas present."

"You bought me something?"

"I know we said we wouldn't exchange gifts, but I couldn't help myself." Maybelle eyed Kat with a wistful smile. "I kept thinking about how you used to beg to open your gifts early when you were small. You would've celebrated Christmas right after Halloween if you could have."

Kat had a vague memory of the sort. She also recalled that the reason she had asked for her gifts early was because she never knew when she would see her mother next.

But that had been a long time ago, back when she was young and hopeful. After several years of her mother giving her things more suitable for someone half her age, she had eventually grown not to care much about presents.

Maybelle was careful not to disturb Tom as she exchanged her coffee mug for her purse. She rummaged through it for a second before holding up a gift-wrapped package. "Here you go."

"What is it?" Although Kat figured she was past the stage of receiving age-inappropriate gifts, after seeing the type of things that made Maybelle happy she wouldn't be surprised if her mother had bought her some brand of moisturizer she didn't care for.

Maybelle tossed the package at her. "Open it and see."

Kat figured she didn't have a choice, but it wasn't until she tore the paper off and saw the container of catnip that she realized how much she had been dreading what she'd find inside.

"The salesclerk at the pet store suggested it," Maybelle said, stroking Tom.

Dazed, Kat turned the container around in her hands. "I thought you weren't a cat person."

"I'm not." Maybelle's fingers danced across Tom's tail. "Although this one is growing on me."

"But why would you buy me this if you don't like cats?"

"Because you like them. You light up when you talk about them on the phone. It makes me happy to hear you so happy, so I thought this might be a way to make all of us happy."

Kat stared at Maybelle. "So you weren't pretending all those times you laughed at my Matty and Tom stories?"

Maybelle's brow furrowed. "Of course not."

Kat hugged the catnip to her chest. Her mother might not know it, but she had just given her the best gift she could have hoped for.

A sharp knock on the door interrupted the moment, turning Kat's blood cold. Andrew had volunteered to work this Christmas, and the look on Maybelle's face told her she wasn't expecting Stephanie or anyone else this afternoon.

That left one, very undesirable visitor as the most likely person to be standing outside her apartment door.

"Well?" Maybelle said, peering at Kat. "Aren't you going to get that?"

Kat's hands were clammy as she placed the catnip on the coffee table. "Maybe we should call Andrew."

"Oh, for goodness' sake." Maybelle jumped off the couch, forcing Tom to sit up. "I'll get it."

Kat's heart lurched. "Maybelle, don't!"

But her mother didn't pay her any heed as she swept across the room. Before Kat could stop her, she flung the door open, not even bothering to peer through the peephole first.

"Hi, I'm looking for Kat," a female voice said.

Kat stood up, the knot in her chest unfurling when she caught sight of the familiar face in the doorway. "Oh, Janice. It's only you."

Janice grinned. "Nice to see you too, Kat."

"I didn't mean it that way." Kat turned toward Maybelle. "This is one of my neighbors, Janice. Janice, this is my mother."

"Nice to meet you, Ms. Harper," Janice said.

"Oh, please, none of this 'Ms. Harper' business," Maybelle said with a scoff. "That makes me sound so old. Call me Kelly—or Maybelle. Your choice."

Janice quirked her lips. Kat would have to explain later why her mother had two names.

Kat extended her arm toward the living room. "Would you like to come in?"

"No thanks. I'm on my way out to see my sister and her family." Janice held up a package. "But this was downstairs for you."

Kat's mouth went dry. "Don't tell me, it's addressed to K. Harper."

"Yup."

"Then it's for me," Maybelle announced, grabbing it from Janice's hands.

"Don't open it," Kat said to her.

"Why on earth not?"

Dumbfounded, Kat could only gape at her mother. Had she already forgotten their conversation with Andrew yesterday? Had she already dismissed the possibility that the person sending her gifts might be dangerous?

Given that she'd answered the door without even bothering to verify who was there, Kat had to guess the answers to those questions was yes.

"You didn't happen to see who left this package, did you?" Kat asked Janice.

Janice shook her head. "It was just propped up outside the main door."

Kat took some comfort from the fact that Maybelle's secret admirer hadn't come inside the building. Even so, the queasy feeling in her stomach wasn't going away. "Have you noticed any strangers hanging around here recently?"

"No." Janice frowned. "Is something going on?"

"Nothing for you to worry about." Kat slapped on the best facsimile of a smile she could muster, figuring there was no point in dampening Janice's Christmas with their troubles. "Thanks for bringing this up."

"Sure." Janice took a step toward the elevator. "Merry Christmas."

"You, too," Maybelle returned, waving with

all five fingers of her free hand.

Kat slammed the door shut, her smile fading as soon as she slid the dead bolt into place. "You are not opening that package." She strode over to the coffee table and snatched up her cell phone. "I'm calling Andrew, and we're going to hand it over to him."

"At least let me read the card," Maybelle said.

Kat was about to tell her no when she heard the unmistakable sound of paper tearing. By the time she turned around, Maybelle had the card in her hands.

"Oh, listen to this," she said. " 'It's hard to be festive when you're not around. Each day I see you is like Christmas to my heart.' "

"Yeah, that's real cute," Kat deadpanned. "Now I'm calling Andrew."

She punched in the proper speed dial number, but something clicked in her brain before she could connect the call. What had her mother and Stephanie said about attending the Apple Blossom Festival way back when? They'd claimed to have gone to the annual Wenatchee event with another friend—a male friend.

Snippets of the notes Maybelle had received flashed through her mind.

. . . *Aplet* of my eye . . .

. . . a spring *blossom* in the winter . . .

. . . hard to be *festive* . . .

Kat sucked in a breath. Were these notes actually veiled references to that long-ago get-together?

"You just went white as a ghost," Maybelle said. "What is it?"

Kat squeezed her phone. "I think I know who your secret admirer is."

CHAPTER TEN

After Kat filled Maybelle in on her theory, Maybelle called Stephanie and got the address. Kat knew they were at the right place when they neared the house.

"There's the silver pickup," Maybelle said, pulling up behind it.

Kat unbuckled her seat belt. "Do you know what you're going to say to him?"

"I'll wing it."

They climbed out of the car and approached the porch. Maybelle did the honors of ringing the bell, and it didn't take long before a handsome, fifty-something man answered. His blue eyes lit up when he saw them.

"Maybelle," he said. "Or, Kelly. You came."

Maybelle jammed her hands on her hips.

"You're the one who's been leaving me all those presents, Jonah?"

He grinned, exposing a gap between his two front teeth. "Did you like them?"

"You had my daughter scared half to death!" Maybelle scolded.

Jonah glanced at Kat. "You're the daughter?"

"Kat Harper," Kat confirmed.

He leaned back to take her in. "Wow, you're all grown up, aren't you?"

"Jonah, we need to talk." Maybelle stormed past him into the house, then spun around. "What on earth were you thinking?"

"I didn't mean to cause you any anxiety," he said, holding the door open for Kat.

"Then why didn't you sign your name?" Maybelle asked.

Kat stepped quietly into the room and stood off to the side. This was her mother's battle, and she planned to stay out of it.

Jonah secured the door before facing Maybelle. "After all the trouble I brought upon you way back when, I didn't know how you felt about me."

"I never blamed you," Maybelle said, her voice softer now.

"But if I'd never gotten you hooked on those

drugs, you wouldn't have lost custody of—" He broke off, shooting Kat a sheepish look.

"That wasn't your fault. We were both so irresponsible back then. We thought we were invincible."

Jonah shoved his hands in his pants pockets. "When I saw you at that gas station, I couldn't believe it. I almost went up to you, but I was shocked speechless. It was like a blast from the past. You haven't changed a bit."

Maybelle fingered her hair. "Oh, now you're just being kind."

"It's true." Jonah gazed into her eyes. "You look exactly like you did when you disappeared all those years ago."

They stared at each other for a long moment, neither one saying a word. Kat shifted her feet, tempted to excuse herself. She felt as though she were intruding on a private moment.

Finally, Maybelle coughed and looked away. "Why did you address those gifts to K. Harper?" she asked.

"You told that gas station clerk your name was Kelly," Jonah said. "That's when I started thinking my eyes were playing tricks on me and maybe you weren't you after all. So I followed you to your apartment, and after you went inside I searched the call box for your name. When I spotted that entry for K. Harper, I gathered you were going by Kelly now."

"Why didn't you just buzz me when you were at the apartment?" Maybelle asked.

"Since you never contacted me after moving back to Cherry Hills, I assumed you were avoiding me on purpose."

"I didn't move back. I'm visiting Kat for the holidays. She lives here."

Jonah rubbed his nose. "And here I thought you were trying to forget me."

"Oh, Jonah." Maybelle grabbed his hand. "I could never forget you."

He smiled at her. "We did have some good times, didn't we? That year at Apple Blossom Festival was the highlight of my life."

Maybelle withdrew her hand, a shadow crossing over her face. "But Jonah, we shared some pretty bad times, too."

"Yes." He bowed his head. "It were those bad times that made me think you might never want to see me again." He peeked up at her, pain in his eyes. "I never should have introduced you to the drugs. Once I got clean, I always kicked myself for that."

"I begged you to let me try it," Maybelle said. "I was so adventurous back then."

"We were both too adventurous for our own good."

"That's for sure." Maybelle scrunched up her nose. "But why all the gifts?"

"I couldn't help myself. After I saw you at that gas station you were constantly on my mind. I kept stumbling across all these things that reminded me of you." He rocked on his heels. "And, I admit, even though I told myself I wouldn't pressure you to see me, I was hoping the messages I left reminded you of how much fun we used to have together and spur you to get in touch."

"You should have signed your name," Maybelle told him.

"I didn't mean to worry you. Or your daughter. And I only bought those things because I thought you would like them."

"I do like them, Jonah. But you know nothing can happen between us. We have too much history. We live in different states." Maybelle's lips puckered. "And you were married to one of my best friends!"

"That's your fault," Jonah said.

Maybelle reared back. "My fault?"

"Stephanie and I were both devastated when you vanished. Our grief brought us closer together, and one day we mistook it for love."

Maybelle stared at him. She seemed to be at a loss for words.

He gave her a weak smile. "You probably don't realize how much I cared for you back then. I had always hoped something romantic would develop between us."

Maybelle lifted her hand to her heart. "I didn't know that."

"I never told you. You were head over heels for Quinn back then."

"I guess I'm partly at fault." Maybelle shifted her gaze to Kat. "I've been told I tend to flirt too much."

Jonah grinned. "It's one of the things I like most about you. You're not afraid to be bold."

"It can get me into trouble, too." Maybelle paused, then added, "I apologize for any grief I caused you."

Jonah flapped his hand. "It's all water under the bridge. Our whole gang was young and foolish." He grimaced. "I might not be young anymore, but I suppose I'm still foolish. I never thought those gifts would scare you."

"They didn't scare me, they scared Kat," Maybelle said. "But why were you following me around in your truck?"

He flushed. "That was a tad impulsive on my part. The first time, after I spotted you at that gas station, I wanted to see if it was really you."

"And what about Christmas Eve morning?"

"I happened to be out and about shopping for my nephews when I saw that little red car of yours on the road again. My curiosity got the better of me, and I started trailing you."

Maybelle swatted his forearm. "Well, you shouldn't have done that."

"I realize that now. It was just so surreal, seeing you in Cherry Hills again. I had to make sure my mind wasn't playing tricks on me."

"Next time pick up the phone if you want to reach me."

Jonah's eyes sparkled. "Does that mean I can call?"

"Yes. I'll give you my number."

Kat watched as they programmed each other's contact information into their cell phones. Jonah had a dreamy look on his face, as if Maybelle had just given him everything he'd ever wanted for Christmas. It might not have been the best decision to leave those anonymous gifts, but Kat believed him when he said he hadn't meant to alarm them.

Maybelle stuffed her phone back into her coat pocket. "Well, Kat and I should take off and let you get on with your Christmas."

Jonah's face fell. "You're leaving so soon?"

"I want to spend some quality time with my daughter today."

Maybelle's words swirled around Kat like a balm, soothing the old childhood wounds she had held on to for so long. She might not be completely healed after this visit, but she at least knew now that her mother was doing her best, just as she had all those years ago.

And, really, wasn't that all anyone could ask for?

Jonah escorted them to the door. Maybelle stopped just past the threshold and reached back to take his hand.

"Nothing romantic will ever happen between us, but you'll always have a special place in my heart," she said.

He pulled her into a hug. "As you will in mine, Maybelle. You realize I think of you every time I eat an ear of corn? I had a knot on my head for two weeks after that old Apple Blossom vendor whacked me with that corncob."

Maybelle threw her head back and laughed. The sound of her happiness filled Kat with a joy that promised to carry her all the way through New Year's.

CHAPTER ELEVEN

The rest of Christmas Day passed in a blur. Maybelle and Kat spent the evening in Kat's apartment, sometimes chatting, sometimes watching movies, but mostly just enjoying each other's company. Before she knew it, it was Saturday morning and Maybelle was all packed to leave in an hour.

They were sitting in the living room sipping coffee and hot chocolate when Larry came up to Kat's apartment. One glimpse at the large box in his arms was all it took for Kat's beverage to threaten a return appearance.

"That can't be for K. Harper," she said.

"Sure is."

Kat slipped her hand into her pants pocket and fingered her cell phone, debating over whether to call Andrew. She had hoped the gifts would stop now that Maybelle had confronted Jonah, but maybe their visit had only fueled his obsession.

Larry took a step forward. "I'll bring it in for you."

"Oh, you don't have to do that." Kat was tempted to tell him to throw it away.

"I insist."

Before she could protest, Larry barreled past her. Spotting the way his chest puffed out when he saw Maybelle, his ulterior motive for being so helpful became a lot clearer.

Maybelle jumped off the couch and twirled a strand of hair around one finger. "Larry!"

"Hey, Maybelle." He grinned. "How was your Christmas?"

Maybelle looked at Kat, a soft smile playing on her lips. "It was magical."

Warmth filled Kat's insides. She couldn't think of a better word to describe it.

"Glad to hear it." Larry set the box on the floor. "Kat here has got herself a late present."

Maybelle bit her lip, and Kat knew she was also thinking about Jonah.

Larry rubbed his palms together. "Well, as much as I'd like to stay and chat with you gals, one of the first-floor residents says his heater's been acting up."

Maybelle walked over and hugged him. "It was good seeing you again."

"You too, Maybelle. We oughta get together before you leave town."

Maybelle pouted as she pulled back from their embrace. "Unfortunately, I'm heading out in an hour."

Larry nodded. "Next time you're in Cherry Hills, then."

"I'd love that."

Larry saluted Kat on his way out. She waved before shutting the door and turning her attention to the box.

"Think it's from him?" she asked Maybelle.

Maybelle shook her head. "Look."

The tension drained from Kat's muscles when she followed the direction of Maybelle's finger to the shipping label she had missed earlier. "It must be that cat tree I ordered."

"Cat tree?" Maybelle's eyes drifted toward Matty and Tom snoozing under the Christmas tree.

"A real cat tree." Kat kneeled on the carpet and started opening the package.

The cats' ears pricked when they heard the sound of tape tearing away from cardboard. They wandered over to see what was going on.

"You'll have to wait until I get it assembled," Kat told them, folding back the box flaps.

Maybelle sat down on the coffee table. "I'll help."

"You don't have to."

"It's the least I can do for ignoring you when Stephanie was here the other day."

"I've been thinking about that," Kat said, keeping her gaze focused on the box, "and maybe I overreacted. It's only natural that you wanted to see your old friends while you were here."

"No, I owe you an apology." Maybelle set her hand on Kat's, forcing her to stop what she was doing. "You want to know the real reason why I kept inviting Stephanie to join us?"

"Because she used to babysit me?"

"Well, yes, there is that, but that's not the only reason. The truth is, the thought of spending time alone with you made me nervous."

Kat dared to meet her mother's eyes. "Nervous?"

"I hadn't seen you in so long, and I still have all this guilt over how I left things between us all those years ago. I try to mask it by being extra cheerful, but it's still there, deep down inside of me. And I know you're not happy with me for leaving back then either. How could you be? You grew up in foster care because of me."

Kat's vision blurred as she stared at her mother's hand on top of hers. Maybelle's words had unleashed a jumble of emotions within her.

Maybelle drew in a breath. "I thought if there was another person around you'd be less likely to give me the dressing down I deserved for abandoning you all those years ago. Stephanie was kind of like . . . I don't know. A buffer, I guess."

"A buffer," Kat repeated, remembering how she had wanted Andrew present three days ago for that exact same reason.

"I know it's silly."

Kat smiled as she blinked away her tears. "It's not silly."

They didn't speak, too busy gazing at each other. Kat was vaguely aware of Matty and Tom orbiting around them as the cats attempted to peek inside the box, but mostly she was just savoring this moment with her mother.

The spell was broken when Matty crawled up Kat's shirt and prepared to use her shoulder as a springboard into the box.

"We should get to work before the cats die of curiosity," Kat said, easing Matty off of her.

Maybelle reached into the box and extracted a carpet-covered perch. "Sounds like a plan."

Kat and Maybelle focused their attention on unpacking. Every time they set a new part on the floor, Matty and Tom moved in to make sure it met their standards. That involved sitting on each piece to verify sturdiness, spotchecking the scratching surfaces, and sniffing out subpar materials.

Just when everything was finally spread out and Kat was ready to begin assembly, Tom decided he needed a break and laid down on the instruction sheet.

"Tom, scoot," Kat said. She turned toward Matty, who was batting at the included Allen wrench with her paw. "Matty, you're not helping."

Maybelle laughed. "I can see why you enjoy having animals around."

Kat raised her eyebrows. "Don't tell me you're turning into a cat person."

"Nah." Maybelle reached over and petted Tom. "But I am growing rather fond of these two."

Kat supposed that was more than she could ask for.

Maybelle scanned the sea of parts surrounding them. "So where do we start?"

Kat lifted up Tom's tail to look at the diagram. "There should be a flat platform somewhere that will serve as the base. It has the number one stamped on the bottom."

Maybelle checked two different pieces before holding one up. "Got it."

"Now we have to find the sisal post."

As if she understood, Matty ran over to the post in question and dug her claws into it.

"Matty, that's going to conk you on the head if you're not careful," Kat said, easing it from the tortoiseshell's grasp.

Kat somehow managed to screw the post to the base without the cats interfering.

"Here's part number three," Maybelle said, handing Kat a triangular hut just large enough to conceal a medium-sized house cat.

"Great." Kat took it from her and secured it to what they had so far.

Matty's patience expired as soon as Kat tightened the last screw. She positioned her front paws on the hut's entryway and pulled herself inside.

"Matty, you're in the way," Kat told her.

Tom abandoned his station on the assembly diagram when he spotted Matty's tail hanging out of the hut. He took a swing at it, sending Matty into a frenzy as she scrambled to turn herself around.

Maybelle leaned back on her hands. "Maybe

we could leave it like this. It looks like they're enjoying it just the way it is."

"That would certainly be easier than trying to work around them," Kat agreed. "But then I'd be left with a bunch of cat tree pieces scattered across my living room floor."

"In that case, let's get back to work."

Thirty minutes later, after much shooing, nudging, and cajoling, the cat tree was fully assembled. Maybelle and Kat stood back to examine their handiwork.

"It looks pretty good, doesn't it?" Maybelle said.

"I don't know," Kat replied. "I think it needs one more thing."

"What's that?"

"A little flavoring." Kat picked up the container of catnip that Maybelle had given her yesterday.

Matty and Tom watched, transfixed, as catnip rained down on their new tree. When Kat was finished, Tom threw himself at the dusting on the bottom level and rolled around as if he had been transported to kitty heaven.

"He likes it," Maybelle said.

Kat's heart swelled as she took in how happy Matty and Tom looked. "Thank you for my Christmas gift." She paused, then added, "I'm sorry I didn't get you anything."

"Seeing you again is the best gift ever."

Kat smiled. Despite their rocky start and a few rough patches along the way, their Christmas had turned out pretty well after all.

Maybelle checked the time on her cell phone. "I should head out before it gets too dark."

"I'll walk you downstairs," Kat said, trying to ignore the ache that blossomed in her chest.

Maybelle slipped on her coat and shoes. "You stay here where it's warm. I know the way."

"Okay."

They stood there for an awkward moment, neither one seeming to know how to end this visit. Then they moved forward at the same time. As their arms snaked around each other, Kat felt as if they were finally in sync.

"I'm so, so glad I got to reconnect with you after all these years," Maybelle murmured in Kat's ear.

Tears welled in Kat's eyes. "I'm glad, too . . . Mom."

Maybelle pulled back, her mouth dropping open. When she reached for Kat again, her second hug was twice as fierce.

"I wish I could stay longer," Maybelle whispered, and Kat could tell from the way her voice wavered that she was struggling not to cry.

"You're always welcome to visit," Kat told her.

"Thank you. And you ought to come down to Estacada one of these days."

"I just might do that."

Maybelle stepped back. Her eyes were moist, and she dabbed at the underside of her eyelids with one finger. "Well, it's time for me to hit the road."

"I'll get the door."

Kat opened the door while Maybelle grabbed her luggage. Maybelle stopped to squeeze Kat's shoulder before she stepped into the corridor.

"Bye, baby."

"Bye, Mom."

Maybelle kept glancing back as she walked down the hallway. When she boarded the elevator, she gave Kat one final departing wave. Kat returned the gesture before heading back inside.

She shut the door and rested her head against it. The ache in her chest was still there, but her heart felt light.

Their visit might be over, but to Kat it felt like just the beginning.

NOTE FROM THE AUTHOR

Thank you for visiting Cherry Hills, home of Kat, Matty, and Tom! If you enjoyed their story, please consider leaving a book review on your favorite retailer and/or review site.

Keep reading for an excerpt from Book Thirteen of the Cozy Cat Caper Mystery series, *Choked in Cherry Hills*, and descriptions of some of the other books in the series. Thank you!

CHOKED *in* CHERRY HILLS

The Furry Friends Foster Families January fundraiser turns fatal when one of the guests ends up murdered. But who would want to kill popular local radio personality John Sykes? Kat Harper doesn't know, but she's running into plenty of people with motive for murder. Now if she could only figure out which one is guilty.

* * *

Please check your favorite online retailer for availability.

CHOKED
in CHERRY
HILLS

COZY CAT

A CAPER

MYSTERY
BOOK

13

PAIGE SLEUTH

Something was coiled around Katherine Harper's neck. She could feel it encircling her throat, cutting off her airway. Whoever was choking her had a hold on her head, keeping her immobilized and helpless. She wanted to scream, but that was impossible when she couldn't draw air into her lungs. Terror spread through every cell in her body. She was only thirty-two, much too young to die.

Kat's eyes flew open in a panic, her heart racing in her chest. Gasping for breath, she reached up to fight off her assailant. Her fingers landed on something soft and warm, something that felt quite familiar.

Tom flicked his tail in her face and adjusted

positions. Kat let out a strangled laugh, her heart starting to return to its normal rate. The attack had been a dream, one perpetuated by a certain big cat's insistence on sleeping on her pillow.

Kat levered herself up on one elbow and turned on the bedside lamp. "I thought you were trying to kill me," she scolded the brown-and-black feline.

Tom pried one eye open. The expression on his face suggested he wasn't above such a deed if he deemed it necessary.

Kat ruffled his fur. "You can't fool me with that tough-guy attitude. I know you're a big softie at heart."

Tom shut his eye and relaxed. Pretty soon, the sound of his purring filled the room.

Kat snuggled closer to Tom while she petted him, savoring this moment for as long as she could. January mornings could be cold in Cherry Hills, Washington, and she would like nothing more than to stay buried under the covers all day.

Unfortunately, she had to start getting ready for work soon.

Kat checked the bedside clock. On the off chance that Matty, her yellow-and-brown tortoiseshell, failed to rouse her for breakfast according to her usual strict schedule, the alarm was programmed to go off in half an hour. Kat moved the knob to the radio setting instead.

"Let's see what John Sykes has to say this morning, shall we?" she suggested to Tom as she adjusted the dial.

She rarely listened to talk radio, but since John Sykes had volunteered to auction off an evening out in his company to benefit Furry Friends Foster Families, she figured she should tune in to the local radio personality's show at least once.

". . . totally agree, Bob," a melodious male voice boomed through the speakers when Kat found the proper frequency. "Fitness is a life-long commitment. Speaking for myself, it can be a challenge to find the time, but this year I'm making a point to show up at the gym at least twice a week. What about you, listeners? Anyone want to join me in my pledge to better health?"

Kat swung her legs out of bed, frowning when she noticed the stiffness in her calves. She couldn't remember the last time she'd been inside a gym.

"For those of you just tuning in, we're talking New Year's resolutions. Have one? Hate 'em? Call in and let us know where you stand."

Tom turned his head toward the radio and meowed his two cents before leaning back to groom his tummy.

"You're not into resolutions either, huh?" Kat replied. She gave Tom's ample stomach a scratch, feeling it yield beneath her fingers. "Or fitness," she added.

The man who Kat presumed was John Sykes came back on the radio. She listened while heading over to the closet to select an outfit for work.

"Happy Friday to all of you just joining us. If this is your first time tuning in this week, I have some exciting news to share with you. Tonight I'll be up north in Cherry Hills for a charity auction. You ever been to Cherry Hills, Eli?"

"Once or twice," a more nasal male voice chimed in. "Can't say the town offered much in terms of entertainment."

"If it's entertainment you want, today's your lucky day. A wonderful little animal rescue there called Furry Friends Foster Families is hosting a silent auction tonight to earn some much-needed funds for those homeless puppies and kitties. And one of the auction items up for bid is a very special evening with yours truly."

"If somebody is desperate enough to fork over cold hard cash to spend time with you, they're welcome to give me a call," Eli quipped. "I'll give 'em this seat right here."

John chuckled. "Now, Eli, we're not letting you sleep in that easily."

Matty sauntered into the bedroom. The tortoiseshell stopped just past the threshold and glanced at the radio.

"And here's the expert at keeping people from sleeping in," Kat said, greeting the feline with a head scratch. "Right on time to beg for breakfast, I see."

Matty let Kat pet her for a few seconds before leaping on top of the mattress. Her ears pricked when she caught sight of the clean slacks Kat had laid out.

"Don't even think about it." Kat snatched her pants off the bed before Matty could shed all over them.

"So, ladies," John Sykes was saying, "now that you have the lowdown, I expect to see a bunch of you in Cherry Hills tonight."

"And remember, if the thought of spending a full evening with John fails to float your boat, there's still plenty of reasons to join us tonight," Eli said. "Lots of other auction items will be up for grabs—ones that are much more appealing than the threat of being stuck with my dud of a co-host for hours on end."

"That's right," John said, laughing. "And all the money is going to a good cause."

Kat smiled as she changed out of her pajamas. She was happy the radio hosts were putting in a good word for the silent auction. She, Imogene Little, and Willow Wu—the three Furry Friends Foster Families board members—had put a lot of work into tonight's fundraiser, and they were banking on it being enough of a success to support the needs of their foster animals for the next few months.

Kat buttoned her slacks and pulled a belt out of the closet. Deciding to have some fun before she put it on, she grabbed hold of the buckle and wiggled the other end at the cats.

Matty's pupils dilated, and she jabbed at the belt with one paw. Tom, on the other hand, didn't want to have anything to do with the snake-like object. He scurried toward the far side of the bed and buried his head under the pillows.

Kat laughed. "You're seriously scared of a little belt? And you're always the first one to attack my shoelaces."

Losing interest in the belt game, Matty trotted over to Tom and licked his neck. Tom flinched, but when he saw it was only Matty he started purring again.

Excerpt from *Choked in Cherry Hills*

Kat's insides warmed. "It must be nice to have a sibling who looks out for you," she said, ignoring the ache she experienced sometimes when she was reminded that she had no brothers or sisters of her own.

Before Kat could become too maudlin, the voices on the radio captured her attention again. The hosts were still discussing the 4F auction.

"You looking forward to tonight, Eli?" John Sykes asked.

"I wouldn't miss it."

"Good. For all you listeners on the fence about driving a little ways to attend a charity auction, let me remind you that I'll be there meeting and greeting everyone in person."

"You're supposed to be encouraging our listeners to show up tonight, not driving them away," Eli joked.

"Well, in that case, I'll offer everyone out there a guarantee. Show up this evening, and I promise I'll make this one of the most memorable nights you'll have this year."

Kat wouldn't realize the truth of his statement for another twelve hours.

* * *

Please check your favorite online retailer for availability.

DROPPED DEAD in CHERRY HILLS

Kat Harper's visit to Jessie's Diner ends abruptly when the man at the next table drops dead. Nobody suspects murder until a wannabe crime reporter and some disturbing evidence convinces them otherwise. Now it's up to Kat to figure out "whodunit."

* * *

Please check your favorite online retailer for availability.

VALENTINE'S
in CHERRY
HILLS

Kat Harper is in for a Valentine's Day surprise when her police detective boyfriend is spotted with another woman. Kat doesn't believe Andrew would cheat on her, but that doesn't explain why he's being so mysterious. If she wants answers she'll have to investigate herself . . . but she better be careful or she might find herself crossing paths with a criminal more dangerous than any she's ever encountered before.

* * *

Please check your favorite online retailer for availability.

DROWNED *in* CHERRY HILLS

Kat Harper's morning workout takes a sinister turn when she discovers a dead body in the gym pool. All evidence points to murder, and Kat can't help but speculate over "whodunit." But she'd better hope the killer doesn't find out about her amateur sleuthing, because this time her cats might not be around to save her.

* * *

Please check your favorite online retailer for availability.

ABOUT THE AUTHOR

Paige Sleuth is a pseudonym for mystery author Marla Bradeen. She plots murder during the day and fights for mattress space with her two rescue cats at night. When not attending to her cats' demands, she writes. She loves to hear from readers, and welcomes emails at: paige.sleuth@yahoo.com

If you'd like to join Paige's readers' group, please visit: http://hyperurl.co/readersgroup

CPSIA information can be obtained
at www.ICGtesting.com
Printed in the USA
BVHW032327150820
586545BV00001B/290